Contents

DAVID A. ADLER

When he was young, David A. Adler dreamed of being a baseball player. But he wasn't a very good hitter. Luckily, he was a good storyteller, so he became a writer instead. David is the author of more than seventy books, including biographies and books of riddles.

SUSANNA NATTI

Susanna Natti has always loved to draw. When she was young, she and her favorite cousin even had their own drawing contests. When Susanna was ten, her art teacher taught her an important rule: Start your picture by drawing the whole shape. Then go back and fill in the details. Susanna still follows that rule every time she draws!

The *Cam Jansen Adventure* series

CAM JANSEN
and the
Mystery of the
Babe Ruth Baseball

DAVID A. ADLER
Illustrated by Susanna Natti

HOUGHTON MIFFLIN COMPANY
BOSTON
ATLANTA   DALLAS   GENEVA, ILLINOIS   PALO ALTO   PRINCETON

Acknowledgments

For each of the selections listed below, grateful acknowledgment is made for permission to excerpt and/or reprint original or copyrighted materials, as follows:

Selections

"The Babe Calls His Shots," from *Baseball's Best: Five True Stories,* by Andrew Gutelle, illustrated by Cliff Spohn. Text copyright © 1990 by Andrew Gutelle. Illustrations copyright © 1990 by Cliff Spohn. Reprinted by permission of Random House, Inc.

Cam Jansen and the Mystery of the Babe Ruth Baseball, by David A. Adler, illustrated by Susanna Natti. Text copyright © 1982 by David A. Adler. Illustrations copyright © 1982 by Susanna Natti. Reprinted by permission of Viking Penguin, a division of Penguin Books USA, Inc.

"The Home Run King," by Robert W. Peterson, from April 1993 *Boys' Life* magazine. Copyright © 1993 by Robert W. Peterson. Reprinted by permission of the author and *Boys' Life,* published by the Boy Scouts of America.

"Hot Hobby: Collecting Baseball Cards," from June 1991 *National Geographic World.* Copyright © 1991 by National Geographic *World.* Reprinted by permission of National Geographic *World,* the official magazine for Junior Members of the National Geographic Society.

Photography

ii Courtesy of David Adler (t); courtesy of Susanna Natti (b). **59** The Bettmann Archive. **60–61** UPI/The Bettmann Archive. **68** Letraset; William Johnson/Johnson's Photography (bm). **70** Atlanta Braves. **72** AP Worldwide Photos, Inc. **74** AP Worldwide Photos, Inc.

1997 Impression
Houghton Mifflin Edition, 1996
Copyright © 1996 by Houghton Mifflin Company. All rights reserved.

Printed in the U.S.A.

ISBN: 0-395-73229-8

789-B-99 98 97

To Bette and Simeon Guterman
with love

Chapter One

It was a Sunday afternoon at the end of May. Cam Jansen and her friend Eric Shelton were in the local community center. A hobby show was being held there, and Cam's parents had brought their collection of circus posters.

Cam's father fixed his bow tie. He looked at his watch and said, "It's almost time."

"You should go now, before you miss it," Cam's mother added.

Cam and Eric rushed to the clock corner, where there were more than twenty cuckoo clocks hanging on the wall. It was almost four o'clock. Cam and Eric waited. Then the noise started. When the minute hand of each clock reached twelve, a tiny door opened and a small wooden bird popped out. "Cuckoo, cuckoo, cuckoo, cuckoo," it chirped.

All the birds seemed to be coming out of all the clocks at once. People in the large room turned to look at the clocks. Many of them looked at their watches to see if it really was four o'clock.

After the clock doors had closed, Cam and Eric looked at some of the other exhibits. They looked at needlepoint pillows, the Collins Coin Shop exhibit, a display of old toys, and at a large collection of baseball cards, yearbooks, and posters.

"Look here," Eric said. "There's a whole section about Babe Ruth."

There were a few Babe Ruth baseball cards, some photographs, a baseball the

Babe had autographed, and a large poster of Babe Ruth hitting a home run. The poster also listed his record as a player.

"Test my memory," Cam told Eric. "Ask me anything about Babe Ruth's playing record."

Cam looked carefully at all the numbers on the poster. Then she closed her eyes and said, *"Click."* Cam always says, *"Click,"* when she wants to remember something. When people ask her why, she points to her head and tells them, "This is a mental camera. Just like any camera, it goes *'click'* when it takes a picture."

"What was the Babe's real name?" Eric asked.

"George Herman Ruth," Cam said with her eyes still closed.

"How many games did he play in 1924?"

"One hundred and fifty-three."

Cam has what people call a photographic memory. Her mind takes a picture of whatever she sees. When she wants to re-member something, even a detail such as how many games Babe Ruth played in any one year, she just looks at the photograph stored in her brain.

Cam's real name is Jennifer Jansen. But when people found out about her amazing memory, they called her "The Camera." Soon "The Camera" was shortened to "Cam."

"When did Babe Ruth get the most hits?" Eric asked.

"In 1923. He had two hundred and five hits that year. And he hit the most home runs in 1927. That's when he hit sixty," Cam said, with her eyes still closed.

The owner of the collection was listening. He was an old man. He had a bushy white mustache, and he was wearing a baseball cap.

"You really know all about baseball," the old man said.

Cam opened her eyes and said, "No, I don't. I just remember everything on that poster."

Then Eric told him, "She has a mental camera. Why don't you test her?"

The old man picked up a box of baseball cards. "Take a card," he called to the people around the exhibit. "We'll see how good this girl's memory *really* is."

Two people reached into the box and took out a card. Cam looked at the people. Then she looked at the cards they were holding. She said, *"Click,"* and closed her eyes.

"What card am I holding?" a teenage boy wearing jeans and a bright green jacket asked.

"You're holding a Reggie Jackson card."

"That's right," the boy said. Then he looked at his card and asked, "How many doubles did he hit in 1977?"

"Thirty-nine."

A girl with long brown hair, holding a large gym bag, asked, "What card am I holding? When was the player born and what's his middle name?"

"It's a Stan Musial card. He was born in 1920, on November twenty-first, and his full name is Stanley Frank Musial."

"Amazing!" the man said as Cam opened her eyes. He told her that his name was Henry Baker, and he asked Cam and Eric if they could come back later. He wanted his wife to meet Cam and test her memory.

"Sure, I can come back," Cam told him.

"Oh, good. Now let me show you my collection."

Mr. Baker showed Cam and Eric his favorite baseball cards. He showed them cards of Billy Martin, Fernando Valen-zuela, Ron Guidry, and Satchel Paige. After that, he led Cam and Eric to the Babe Ruth corner.

He showed them his Babe Ruth cards. Then Mr. Baker said, "Wait till you see this. I have a baseball that Babe Ruth signed for me almost fifty years ago."

Mr. Baker turned around. The wooden stand the baseball had rested on was there, but the baseball was gone.

Chapter Two

"Someone stole my baseball!" Mr. Baker cried out.

A woman nearby looked at him. She laughed and said, "Ask your mommy to get you another one."

"This wasn't just any baseball. Babe Ruth signed it. He gave it to me when I was a boy. It's very valuable."

Mr. Baker ran from one person to the next, asking, "Have you seen my baseball? Did you see it rolling on the floor? Did you see someone take it?"

Eric looked on the floor for the ball. Cam stood on a chair to watch what Mr. Baker was doing.

"He's so upset," Cam told Eric. "He's stopping everyone. Most of them think he's crazy."

While Cam stood on the chair, she looked across the exhibit hall. She saw her parents with a large circus poster hanging behind them. She saw the wall of cuckoo clocks. Then she saw someone leaving the exhibit hall. It was a teenage boy wearing a bright green jacket. Cam closed her eyes and said, *"Click."*

"Let's go!" Cam shouted to Eric when she opened her eyes. "Someone's leaving the hall, and he might have the baseball."

Cam ran between two women trading rare postage stamps. She crawled under a few tables and almost knocked over a small boy looking at some old toys.

Eric followed Cam. "I'm sorry. Excuse me," he said to the two women and the small boy as he hurried past.

When Cam got to the door she told the guard, "You have to stop him!"

"What are you talking about?"

"That boy in the green jacket. He was

there when a valuable baseball was stolen. The baseball was in the exhibit, and I'm sure that boy took it. That's why he's in such a rush to get out of here."

"Just because he's leaving the hall doesn't mean he's a thief," the guard said.

The boy in the green jacket turned and saw Cam talking to the guard. He started to run.

"Did you see that!" Eric said. "He saw us talking to you and he started to run."

The boy ran around the corner of the building. He was out of sight.

"We'll never catch him now," Cam said.

"Yes, we will," the guard said.

He ran after the boy. Cam and Eric followed him.

They ran to a crowded playground on the other side of the building. Two young children were playing catch with a baseball. Others were jumping rope or playing basketball. In one corner of the playground some parents were watching very young children playing in a large sandbox, on seesaws, or on swings.

The guard ran with Cam and Eric until they got to the other end of the playground.

"He's gone," Cam said. "I don't see him anywhere."

They looked down the street leading

from the playground. A few children were walking there. A man was pushing a baby carriage, and there were some people waiting at the bus stop. But no one was wearing a bright green jacket.

"There's another way out of the playground," the guard said. He turned and started to walk toward the other exit. Then he stopped.

"Is that him?" the guard asked, pointing to a boy sitting on one of the park benches.

Chapter Three

The boy sitting on the bench was wearing jeans and a bright green jacket. He was sitting behind the two children who were playing catch.

"Yes, that's him," Cam said.

Cam, Eric, and the guard ran to the bench. The boy looked up at them. He smiled and said, "Well, look who's here. It's the girl with the amazing memory and her quiet friend."

"A valuable baseball is missing from one

of the exhibits," the guard told the boy. "We're looking for it."

"I'm sorry, but I don't know where it is."

Cam looked at the boy. There was something in one of his jacket pockets. It was round and about the size of a baseball.

Cam closed her eyes and said, *"Click."* She looked at the picture in her mind of the boy when he was holding the Reggie Jackson baseball card.

Cam opened her eyes and said, "What's that in your pocket? It wasn't there before."

"Oh, this," the boy said, and reached into his pocket. "You just didn't notice it."

He took out a baseball and showed it to the guard.

"This can't be the missing baseball," the guard said. "It's not signed by Babe Ruth. It says 'Little League Slugger.'"

The guard turned to Cam and Eric and said, "I don't know why I listened to you. Maybe there never was any Babe Ruth baseball. Now I have to get back to the exhibit hall. But first I think you owe this boy an apology."

Cam and Eric told the boy that they were sorry. The guard walked back to the exhibit hall. Cam and Eric walked to a bench on the other side of the playground and sat down.

Cam and Eric lived next door to each

other. They were in the same fifth grade class, and they spent a lot of time together. Eric knew that Cam wouldn't give up the search for the missing baseball so quickly. She didn't.

"Where did he get that ball? He didn't have it when we saw him at Mr. Baker's exhibit."

"Maybe he found it," Eric said.

"Maybe."

Cam closed her eyes. She said, *"Click."* Then she added, "I'm trying to remember everything I saw at the exhibit."

While Cam's eyes were closed, Eric looked around the playground. He saw a side door to the exhibit hall open.

"Cam, look! Isn't that the girl we saw at Mr. Baker's exhibit?"

Cam opened her eyes. She looked at the girl leaving the exhibit hall. The girl had long brown hair and was carrying a gym bag.

"Yes. That's her. And there's enough room in that gym bag for twenty baseballs. I'll bet she left through the side door so no one would see her."

The girl walked past Cam and Eric, but she didn't notice them. She walked out of the playground. At the corner she crossed the street and walked toward the bus stop.

"Come on," Cam said. "Let's follow her."

Cam and Eric had to wait at the corner for the traffic light to turn green. As they waited, the girl got farther and farther ahead. When the light changed, Cam and Eric ran to get closer. The girl turned and saw them. She began running, too.

The girl held the gym bag with both hands as she ran. She ran past the bus stop. She turned and saw Cam and Eric behind her. She looked scared.

At the corner the girl quickly looked to see if any cars were coming. Then she ran across the street.

"Let's rest," Eric said to Cam when they reached the corner.

"No. We have to catch her. I'm sure she took the baseball. That's why she's running."

Cam and Eric crossed the street and chased the girl. She was halfway down the block when her gym bag dropped from her

hands. The girl tripped over the bag and fell.

Cam and Eric caught up with the girl. She was still lying on the sidewalk. The girl held her gym bag up and said, "Here, take what you want. Just don't hurt me."

Chapter Four

"We're not going to hurt you," Eric told the girl.

Cam took the bag from the girl's hands and said, "We're just going to take the Babe Ruth baseball you stole and give it back to Mr. Baker."

"I didn't steal any baseball."

"Then why were you running?"

"I was running because you were chasing me."

"We'll see," Cam said as she opened the bag.

"Wait," Eric said. "It's her bag. We can't look through it unless she says we can."

The girl sat up and said, "Look all you want. You'll see that I didn't steal anything."

Cam reached into the bag. She took out an old newspaper, a puzzle book about outer space, and a dried-up slice of cheese.

"You should really wrap cheese in plastic or foil," Eric told the girl.

Cam reached into the bag again and took out an apple, an empty soda can, and a roller skate. She felt along the bottom of the bag.

"There's no baseball in here, but there sure are a lot of papers."

"Maybe my book report is in there. I wrote it last week, but I can't remember where I put it."

Eric helped the girl up. Cam gave the gym bag back to her and said, "I'm sorry we chased you. And I'm sorry we thought you stole that baseball."

"That's all right," the girl said as she looked through the papers in her bag. "It will be worth it if I find that book report."

The girl took old comic books, crushed homework papers, and candy wrappers from the bag. Cam and Eric left her and started walking toward the exhibit hall. When they reached the corner, the girl waved some papers at them and called out, "I found it! I found it!"

"I'm glad we helped find *something*," Cam said to Eric. "But I wish it had been the baseball."

When Cam and Eric reached the playground, they sat down on one of the benches. Eric watched the children playing basketball.

Cam closed her eyes and said, *"Click."* She thought for a moment. She said, *"Click,"* a few more times. Then she opened her eyes.

"The baseball was there when we first came to the exhibit, but it was gone a few minutes later. So it must have been taken while we were there," Cam said. "I just wish I had a picture of who was standing in the Babe Ruth corner when the ball was taken."

Eric wasn't looking at Cam while she talked to him. He was looking across the playground.

"The one thing that I don't understand," Eric said, "is why that boy ran from the hall. He was in a real hurry then, but he didn't go anywhere. He's still sitting there on that bench."

Cam looked across the playground. Then she closed her eyes and said, *"Click."*

Cam told Eric, "I'm looking at the picture

I have of him at the exhibit. He said he had a baseball in his pocket the whole time, but that's not true. He didn't have it in his pocket when we first saw him."

Cam opened her eyes and asked, "What is he doing over there?"

"It looks like he's watching those two children playing catch."

Cam looked across the playground at the boy in the green jacket. She thought for a minute. Then she clapped her hands together and said, "That's it! I think I know where the Babe Ruth baseball is."

"Where?"

Cam started to explain, but then she saw something that made her stop.

"Look at that," she said, and pointed across the playground. "Now I *know* where the baseball is."

31

Chapter Five

Cam was pointing to the two children playing catch. One of them had thrown the ball too far. The boy in the green jacket was picking it up.

"Did you see that?" Cam asked.

"See what?"

"He picked up their baseball. Now I bet he'll switch baseballs. He'll throw back the one he has in his pocket."

The boy in the green jacket turned around. As he turned, he took the baseball out of his pocket and threw it over his head

to the two children. Then he started to walk away.

"Come on, Eric. Let's follow him."

"Why? What's the difference if he did switch baseballs? Those children couldn't have the Babe Ruth ball. They were outside when it was stolen."

The boy in the green jacket walked quickly away from the playground. He didn't even look as he crossed the street.

Horns honked. Two cars stopped short to avoid hitting him. But the boy didn't even turn around.

Cam ran through the playground and out the exit. Eric followed her. They waited at the corner and then crossed the street when they were sure no cars were coming. The boy was almost a full block ahead of them.

"Let's be careful," Cam told Eric. "I don't want that boy to know we're following him."

Cam and Eric stayed about half a block behind the boy. They walked past a row of stores. At the corner the boy turned around. He looked straight at Cam and Eric.

"Quick!" Cam said. "Let's go into one of these stores."

It was Sunday. The only place open was a small food store. Cam opened the door, and Eric quickly followed her inside.

"Can I help you?" a man behind the counter asked.

"No. We don't need anything," Cam told him.

"Of course you do. Now try to remember what your mother sent you to get. Was it milk? We have regular milk, ninety-nine-

percent-fat-free milk, skim milk, and buttermilk."

"We don't need milk," Eric said.

"Maybe you came for bread or canned vegetables. We have peas, spinach, corn, carrots, and lima beans."

Cam opened the door and looked outside. Then she told Eric, "Let's go before we lose him."

"Maybe you need juice," the man called as Cam and Eric were leaving. "We have orange juice, apple juice, tomato juice, grapefruit juice, and lemon juice."

When Cam and Eric stepped outside the store, they looked for the boy. He was gone. They ran to the corner. They looked ahead and down both side streets.

"There he is," Eric said.

The boy was walking down one of the side streets. Cam and Eric were careful not to get too close. There were a few stores along the first half of the block. The rest of

the block was lined with apartment buildings. They saw the boy walk into one of the
buildings.

Cam and Eric ran to the building. They
peeked into the lobby. The boy was standing there waiting for the elevator. He got
into the elevator, and the doors closed behind him.

Cam and Eric ran into the building.
They watched the numbers over the
elevator door light up. Number five stayed
lit for a long time.

"He got off on the fifth floor," Cam told
Eric. "Now we know where he lives. I'll stay
here and watch to make sure he doesn't
leave. You go get the police."

"No!"

"No?"

"You still haven't told me why we followed him. What will I tell the police?"

Cam sat on one of the chairs in the
lobby. Eric sat next to her.

"While we were sitting in the playground, I looked at the pictures I have
stored in my head. That boy didn't have a
ball in his pocket when we first saw him at
the exhibit. But he did have one when we
saw him later."

"But it wasn't the Babe Ruth baseball."

38

"I know it wasn't. At first that confused me. Then I saw a ball get away from those two children playing catch. When the boy picked it up, I knew what had happened."

"What?"

"That boy took the Babe Ruth ball from the exhibit. He saw us speaking to the guard so he ran. But then he had a better idea. The ball the two children were playing with must have landed near him. That was the first time he switched the baseballs. The two children didn't know it, but they were playing catch with a very valuable baseball."

Eric stood up and said, "Then, while we were watching, he switched the baseballs again. Now he has the Babe Ruth ball."

Eric walked toward the door. As he was leaving the building, he said to Cam, "You wait right here. I'll go and get the police."

"And tell my parents where I am," Cam said.

Cam waited until she was sure that Eric was gone. Then she walked over and pushed the button for the elevator. When it came, she got on and pressed the button for the fifth floor.

Chapter Six

The elevator stopped on the third floor. A woman was standing there reading a flier about the items on sale at the local supermarket. She got into the elevator and asked, "Are you going down?"

"No. I'm going up," Cam answered.

The woman smiled and said, "That's all right. I'll come along for the ride."

The doors closed and the elevator started to move.

The elevator stopped on the fifth floor and Cam got off. The hall was lined with doors. *What will I tell the police?* Cam wondered. *How will they know which is the boy's apartment?*

Cam looked at the names on each of the doors: Benson, Jackson, Goldwin, Cruz, Washington, Hamada, Grant, and Keller.

Maybe his name is Benson, Cam thought. *He looked like a Benson. Or maybe he's a Keller.*

A door opened. It was the door to the Goldwin apartment. As the door opened, a

paper fell to the floor. It was a flier just like the one the woman in the elevator had had. Cam looked at a few of the other apartment doors. Each one had a folded flier pressed into the frame of the door.

A tall woman with red hair just like Cam's came out of the Goldwin apartment. Two children were with her. One of the children, a small boy with curly blond hair, picked up the flier. As they walked to the elevator, the woman smiled at Cam.

Cam waited until they were in the elevator. Then she walked from one apartment door to the next. Two of them, the Goldwins' and the Grants', did not have fliers.

His name is Grant, Cam said to herself. *He must have taken the flier when he went inside.*

Cam was just about to knock on the door when she heard some people get off the elevator. It was Cam's parents and Eric, with a policeman and a policewoman.

"Why didn't you wait for us downstairs?" Eric asked.

"His name is Grant," Cam told them. "This is his apartment."

"What were you about to do?" Cam's father asked.

"I hope you weren't going to knock on the door," Cam's mother said. "Chasing and catching a thief isn't something children should do. It's a job for the police."

The policeman knocked on the door.

"Who is it?" a voice called from inside the apartment.

"It's the police. We'd like to ask a few questions."

The door was opened by a boy wearing jeans.

"Is this the boy you think took the baseball?" the policeman asked.

"Yes," Cam told him.

"No!" the boy shouted. "You're wasting your time. This is the second time these

44

two kids have said I stole that baseball. I
had one with me when I left the exhibit,
but it wasn't the Babe Ruth ball. I showed it
to them the last time."

"Would you please show it to us?" the
policewoman asked.

"Just a minute."

The boy opened a closet near the front door of the apartment. Then he held out a baseball.

Cam looked at the ball. She closed her eyes and said, *"Click."*

"This isn't the same one you showed us in the park," Cam said when she opened her eyes.

"Is this the Babe Ruth baseball?" the policewoman asked.

"No."

"Then let's go."

The boy was just closing the apartment door when something green caught Cam's eye. The boy's jacket was hanging over the back of a kitchen chair. And there was something on the kitchen table.

"Wait," Cam said. "Don't close the door."

Chapter Seven

Cam's father held the door open.

"What is it now?" the policewoman asked Cam.

"I saw the baseball. It's on the kitchen table."

"Are you sure?"

"I think I'm sure."

The policewoman looked inside the apartment. "Oh, there *is* a baseball on the table," she said. "Bring it here," she told the boy.

The boy walked slowly to the kitchen. He

took the baseball off the table and brought it to the policewoman.

"It sure is old," the policewoman said as she looked at the ball. "And it says here 'To Henry Baker, from The Babe.' "

"Maybe it's mine," the boy said.

"Is it?" the policewoman asked.

"Well, no," the boy said softly. "I took it from the old man. I'm sorry."

"You'll have to come to the police station with us. We'll call your parents," the policewoman said as she led the boy to the elevator.

"But first we'll stop at the exhibit," the policeman said. "We'll return the baseball to Mr. Baker."

They all squeezed into the police car. The boy just stared quietly out of the car window. But the police officers and Cam's parents weren't quiet at all. They talked all during the ride to the exhibit hall.

"I'm too young to remember the great

Babe Ruth," the policewoman said. "But my father told me lots of stories about him.

"His favorite story was about the time Babe Ruth hit a home run in the 1932 World Series. The score was tied. There were two strikes. The Babe pointed to the centerfield fence. Then . . ." She paused.

"And then what happened?" asked Cam's mother.

"That's where he hit the very next pitch, right over the centerfield fence."

"And on the *next* pitch," the policeman said, "Lou Gehrig hit a home run."

"He was a pretty good ballplayer, too," Cam's father said.

When they reached the exhibit hall, Cam, her parents, Eric, and the police-woman went inside. Cam held the baseball with both hands.

Mr. Baker was sitting in the Babe Ruth corner of the exhibit. His head was down.

50

Eric tapped him on the shoulder. Then
Cam gave him the baseball.

"You found it! You found it!" Mr. Baker
yelled. He hugged Cam, Cam's father, Eric,
the policewoman, and a man who just happened to be walking past.

"Look, they found my baseball!" Mr.

Baker told his wife when she came from the other side of the exhibit.

"I'm not putting this back on display," Mr. Baker said as he put the baseball in his pocket. "Someone else might take it."

"I want you to come to the station house and sign a complaint against the boy who took it," the policewoman said. "Come as soon as the exhibit closes."

The policewoman started to leave.

"Wait," Mr. Baker said. He took a handful of baseball cards from the box. "Take this," he said as he handed the policewoman a card. "It's Hank Aaron. He's the greatest home run hitter of all time. And here's George Brett and Yogi Berra and Willie Mays and Pete Rose."

The policewoman held up her hands and said, "Oh, thank you, but don't give them to me. Give them to these two children. They're the ones who found your baseball."

Mr. Baker gave the cards to Cam and Eric.

"Can you stay a little longer?" he asked Cam. "My wife would like to see you and your amazing mental camera at work."

"Sure."

"Good. Wait right here. I want everyone to see what a great memory you have."

Chapter Eight

"May I have your attention, please," a woman's voice called out over the loudspeaker. "First, I want to thank you for coming to our hobby show. And I want to invite all of you to go to Henry Baker's baseball exhibit. An amazing memory show will be given there in just a few minutes."

A small crowd gathered around Mr. Baker's exhibit. Cam's parents stood right near the front. Both of them were tall and thin. Cam's father had red hair just like

Cam. Cam's mother's hair was brown and curly.

Mr. Baker and Cam were standing on chairs. Mr. Baker quietly asked Cam a few questions. Then he announced, "The girl standing next to me is Jennifer Jansen. She is in the fifth grade, and she has a remarkable memory."

Mr. Baker picked up a box and said, "I'm going to pick a few cards from this box. Jennifer will take a quick look at the cards. Then I'll let you test her memory."

Mr. Baker picked out some cards and handed them to Cam. Cam said, *"Click,"* as she looked at each card. Then she gave the cards to Eric and closed her eyes.

Eric gave the cards to people in the crowd. "Ask her anything you want," Eric told them.

"I'm holding a Dave Winfield card," someone called out. "What's his middle name?"

"Mark."

"What's Eddie Murray's hobby?"

"Basketball."

A woman standing next to Cam's parents said, "She sure has an amazing memory."

Cam's mother told the woman, "She's our daughter. We're very proud of her."

"And not just because of her memory," Cam's father said. "We were proud of her even before she said her first *'Click.'*"

The Babe Calls His Shot

by
Andrew Gutelle

It's the third game of the 1932 World Series.
The mighty New York Yankees have come to
Chicago to play the Cubs. The Yankees have
already won the first two games of the Series.
The Cubs must win today if they are to have
any chance at all of becoming world champs.

Fifty thousand loyal Cub fans pack
Wrigley Field. They know that the Yankees
and their fans heckled and
embarrassed the
Cubs in New York.
Now it's their turn.
The Chicago rooters
have prepared a
nasty welcome for
the Yankees and
especially for the
greatest Yankee of
them all — Babe Ruth.

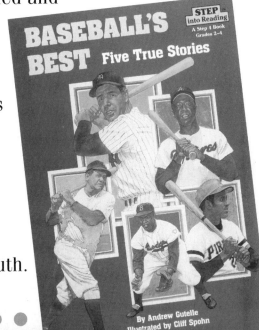

BASEBALL'S
BEST Five True Stories

STEP
into Reading
A Step 4 Book
Grades 2–4

By Andrew Gutelle
Illustrated by Cliff Spohn

George Herman Ruth has been playing major-league ball since 1914. As a pitcher, Babe helps hurl the Boston Red Sox to two world championships. But what really catches everyone's attention is his hitting. Babe can sock a baseball out of sight!

When Ruth is traded to the Yankees, he moves from the pitcher's mound to the outfield and takes New York City by storm. So many fans want to see him play that after a few years the team builds a new, bigger ballpark. In the very first game there the Babe drills a game-winning homer into the upper deck. No wonder everyone soon starts calling Yankee Stadium "The House That Ruth Built."

Babe Ruth, 1930.

Babe Ruth warming up
at Yankee Stadium, 1942
(opposite page).

Ruth is baseball's first superstar. His
cocky and confident style has made him the
most colorful player ever to step into the
batter's box. But some claim that he is
getting old and is no longer the player he
once was. Fans wonder whether he will be
able to make the difference in this crucial
game.

Now, as the Yankees take the field in their
showdown with the Cubs, the crowd boos
Ruth. But the Babe just laughs. He and
teammate Lou Gehrig take batting practice.
As the Cub fans watch, the two sluggers
knock one ball after another into the
bleachers. This show of Yankee power makes
the fans madder. When the Babe trots out to
left field to warm up, the fans hurl lemons at
him. "Get off the field, old-timer!" they shout.

The game begins. In the very first inning Ruth shows what he's got left. He smacks a home run to put the Yankees ahead 3–0. But the Cubs fight back. In the fourth inning a Cub batter hits a sinking line drive to left field. Babe races in and tries to catch the ball before it bounces. To the delight of the crowd, the ball rolls past him for a double. That helps the Cubs tie the score. Suddenly the outcome of the game — and the Series — is in doubt.

In the fifth inning Ruth is again at bat. The crowd is roaring at him. The Cub players are shouting from the bench, too. Ruth looks up at the stands, calm and cool as ever. The first pitch from Charlie Root is a strike. But Ruth does not swing. Instead, he holds up a finger as if to say, "That's one." Soon Root zips another strike past Ruth. Now Babe holds up two fingers. One more strike to go.

The crowd is really going wild. Ruth shouts something at the Cubs' bench. He seems to be pointing to a flagpole in the center-field bleachers. It's as if he's saying to the pitcher, "I'm going to drill the next ball you throw into the bleachers, and you can't stop me!"

Ruth steps back into the batter's box. Root goes into his wind-up. He pitches. Ruth swings and there is a loud crack! The ball blasts off Ruth's bat. Like a rocket it soars to center field. The ball sails into the bleachers and lands a few feet from the flagpole. It has gone just where the Babe said it would!

Ruth circles the bases. For a moment the stunned crowd is silent. Then Yankee fans *and* Cub fans rise to their feet and applaud.

They can't help themselves. Ruth has performed an incredible feat. Does any other player have such nerve or talent? He has challenged the Cubs and their fans and won. The Yankees go on to take the game. The next day they win again to sweep the Series.

"Suppose you hadn't connected?" a reporter asks Ruth after the game.

"I never thought of that," says Babe. "I surely would have looked like a fool."

HOT HOBBY

COLLECTING BASEBALL CARDS

They're colorful, packed with action, and cheap. You can play games with them, make trades with them, or hold on to them and watch them grow in value. They're baseball cards, and collecting them is one of America's fastest-growing hobbies.

Who's buying?

Here are some statistics:

- More than one million people of all ages buy old and new cards.
- Kids ages 7 to 16 buy most new cards.
- Each year more than ten billion cards are produced.

Why buy? A pack of top-of-the-line baseball cards costs a little more than a dollar. Many collectors buy packs for the thrill of opening the wrappers and finding their favorite players. Most know that someday their collections might be worth a lot of money.

Hard-Hitting
Collecting Tips

Collectors Nathan Haas, 14, on the left, and his brother, Ryan, 11, of Bedford, New Hampshire, talk over a trade. As they check a monthly price guide, Nathan points out a crease in a card, which lowers its value. The two try to keep their cards in mint, or top, condition. Here are some tips to get you started on *your* collection.

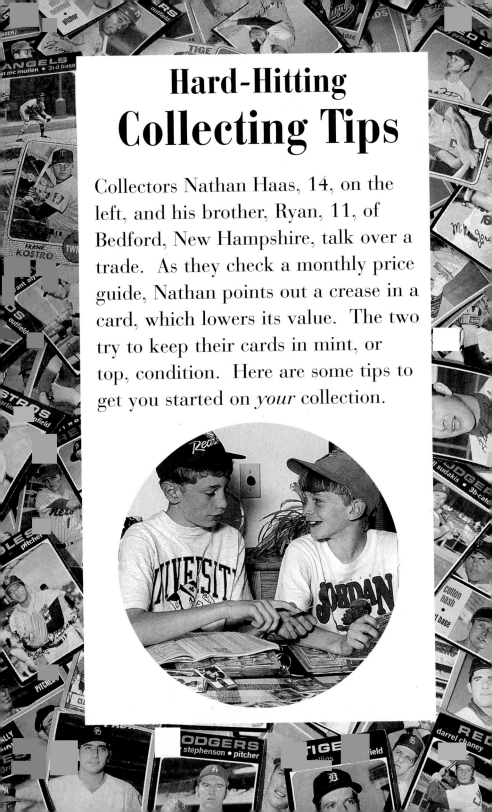

Since you want a collection to give you pleasure, use your imagination in deciding what to collect. You might try to find outstanding pitchers, players who never homered, or players who were born in your home state. Even if your favorite player is Mr. Nobody, save his card. Save the cards of your favorite team, too. Know who the stars are, and save their cards. Hold on to rookie cards, especially those of promising players. If the player on the card becomes a star, that card will gain value.

Keep your cards safe. A card's value depends partly on how old, how rare, and how well kept it is. Put your cards in a binder with plastic sleeves or in a storage box that fits them. Keep them out of sunlight. Avoid damp or hot conditions. Handle them carefully to prevent creasing or bending.

Get organized. Know what you have. Use a baseball card price guide to check the value of your cards. Make a checklist of what you need. Keep it with the price guide and take both to card shops and shows. If you want a card, buy it or trade for it. Shop carefully, compare prices, and don't forget to look at garage sales.

THE HOME RUN KING

by Robert W. Peterson

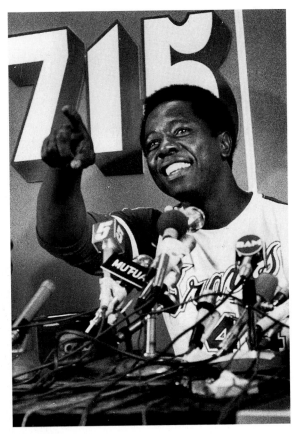

At the press conference after the game in which he hit his historic 715th career home run, a happy Aaron fields questions from one of the nearly 300 reporters assembled there.

Who is the greatest hitter in baseball history?

Some experts would say the legendary Babe Ruth.

Others might argue for Ty Cobb, Ted Williams or Stan Musial. Great hitters, all.

But perhaps the strongest claim to being the best belongs to Hank Aaron. Over 23 years in the major leagues, he set more lifetime marks than anybody.

When Aaron retired after the 1976 season, he stood first for home runs with 755. The runner-up is Babe Ruth with 714. Aaron also had more runs batted in and more total bases than anyone else.

POWER AT THE PLATE

Hank Aaron was not a giant. He stood six feet tall and weighed 180 pounds. But he had very strong hands, wrists and forearms. He batted right-handed, standing deep in the batter's box with his bat held high behind his head. When Aaron swung, he snapped at the ball and sprayed line drives to all parts of the baseball field.

Aaron grew up in Mobile, Alabama, where he was a Boy Scout in Troup 235 of the Ebenezer A.M.E. Zion Church.

Hank Aaron's Records

First for:
Home runs—755
Total bases—6,856
Runs batted in—2,297
Extra-base hits—1,477

Aaron is tied for second with Babe Ruth for runs scored, with 2,174; third for total hits, with 3,771; and eighth for doubles, with 624.

Hank Aaron, the home run king.

At age 18, he was offered $200 a month to play infield with the all-black Indianapolis Clowns. The year was 1952.

After just two months, his contract was sold to the Eau Claire (Wisconsin) Braves of the Northern League. Eau Claire was a farm team of the Boston Braves—now the Atlanta Braves.

Aaron hit so well there that he was named the league's Rookie of the Year. The next year he moved up to a higher minor league and won the league's Most Valuable Player award.

Though already a great hitter, Hank Aaron made a lot of errors in the infield. So, before joining the big leagues in 1954, he moved to the outfield. As a Milwaukee Brave, he won a Gold Glove award for his defensive skills. (The Braves moved to Atlanta in 1966.)

As a power hitter, Hank Aaron's secret was his consistency. For 20 straight years he hit 20 or more homers. He never had more than 47 in a season, although he led the National League four times.

A HISTORIC HOMER

Hank Aaron tied Babe Ruth's mark on opening day of the 1974 season in Cincinnati. A few days later, on April 8, baseball had a new home run king. Aaron hit No. 715 off left-hander Al Downing of the Los Angeles Dodgers.

In his last two seasons, Hank Aaron was with the Milwaukee Brewers of the American League. His final homer—No. 755—came on July 20, 1976, against the California Angels.

But Aaron didn't leave baseball completely. Today he works for the Atlanta Braves as senior vice president and as assistant to the president of the club.

Lots of heavy hitters have followed Hank Aaron. But his standing as the home run king won't be challenged any time soon.

Hank Aaron watches his record 715th home run sail across Atlanta Stadium.